D0095356

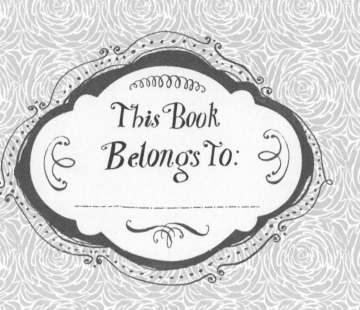

This Book
Belongs To:

THE
MOUSE
WRITER

A Story by Ethan Johnson
Illustrated by Jon Cannell

HUXLEY was a quiet little mouse who kept mostly to himself. He lived alone in a cozy apartment beneath the stairs inside the Taylor family's house. He had a bed, a chair, a couch, and a simple desk where he wrote his stories.

His bookshelves were lined with notebooks he had filled with adventures about his life, stories he'd never shared. He wrote about finding a tasty bit of cheese, meeting a friendly squirrel, or escaping the cat by squeezing through a crack in the wall. Sometimes he wrote outside the apartment, but Tubbs, the cat, made that difficult.

One day Huxley was in the family's living room near the Christmas tree, writing in the only notebook he had left. Suddenly he felt the presence of something large behind him.

OH, NO,

**HUXLEY THOUGHT.
IT'S TUBBS. I MUSTN'T
BECOME LUNCH.**

He dashed down the hall and raced under the table. The cat lost his footing on the shiny wood floor and ran right into a table leg. WHACKKK!

"MEEOWWWCHH,"

Tubbs screeched as he rolled on the floor.

Huxley dived into his apartment. Once inside, he thought, *I've left my notebook. I've got to go back and get it.*

But with Tubbs out there, it wasn't safe. *I guess it's time for my nap,* he thought.

Huxley awoke later that evening and peeked his head out of his apartment. Seeing that there was no cat, he crept into the living room. But the notebook was no longer there. Huxley looked up and saw Griffin, the young boy, reading it on the couch.

"Would you look at this," Griffin said. "It has fantastic stories in it."

"Give me that," said his older sister, Maggie, grabbing the notebook from him.

"WHERE'D YOU GET THIS, GRIFFIN?"

"It's mine. I've always had it."

"No, you haven't," Maggie said. "Where'd you find it?"

"I found it right here on the floor next to the fire," Griffin said.

"Well, it's mine now," Maggie said. She began to read it aloud.

Huxley was astonished to hear his story and to see the joy it brought the children. But as much as he enjoyed listening to Maggie read, he wanted his notebook back. It could be months before he found enough coins under the couch or outside on the sidewalk to purchase another one.

How will I get it? I can't ask for my notebook, he thought. Being a mouse, he knew the children might catch him and put him in a cage or chase him out of the house with a broom. That's when he decided to leave them a little note.

On the kitchen floor, he found a paper napkin. He dipped his tail into the ink bottle he kept in his vest pocket, and wrote a short note:

Please give my give my notebook back.

Sincerely,

Huxley

He left the note on the kitchen counter, hoping that someone would see it. Hidden from sight, he waited for a long time. Eventually Maggie picked it up.

"Did you write this, Griffin?"

"It wasn't me," Griffin said.

"Then who wrote it?"

"Well, Huxley did. Maybe he's a ghost," Griffin said.

Maggie looked angry. "If you're trying to scare me, it's not working. I'm not giving you the notebook, Griffin."

Griffin shook his head. "Who do you suppose Huxley is?"

"Whoever he is, he's going to have to take the notebook from me," Maggie said. "I'm keeping it forever. It has all kinds of fun adventures."

"Let me see it," Griffin said, reaching for the notebook Maggie flashed before him.

"Get your paws off it," Maggie said and walked away.

This is not going well, Huxley thought. *Maybe I haven't asked nicely enough.*

The next day, Huxley found that if he pulled on the toilet paper roll, he could write a much longer message.

This is certain to work, he thought.

I am missing a

It is the only

write my stories in

return it to me,

P.S. I am not a ghost and
I don't mean to frighten you.

small red notebook.

thing I have to
If you would please
I would be
much obliged.

Sincerely,
Huxley

He placed the note on the hallway floor and waited for the children to come home from school. It wasn't long before Griffin opened the front door and walked inside with Maggie trailing behind. Griffin was putting his backpack down when he saw the note. He read it and dropped his books.

"THE GHOST IS BACK!"

Maggie took the note from him. "Someone has been here, all right," Maggie said. "But I don't think it's a ghost."

"Then who is it?" Griffin asked.

"I don't know," Maggie said. She looked around the room. "It could be a leprechaun, I suppose."

"A leprechaun?" Griffin shuddered. "Don't you think we should just put the notebook back by the fire?"

"Don't be ridiculous," Maggie said. "I'm going to keep it and catch my very own leprechaun."

This is not working, Huxley thought.

For the next few days, he left more notes around the house, but each time the children found them they still didn't return his notebook. He decided there was only one thing left to do and that was to talk to the family directly. Not with a note, but face to face. Man to mouse.

That evening as the family ate supper, Huxley climbed onto the dining table. He was hiding behind a large serving bowl filled with mashed potatoes, trying to work up his nerve, when someone took away the serving dish. He was suddenly in full view of the wide-eyed family.

This is when Huxley realized there is nothing a family hates worse than seeing a mouse on the dinner table. *Well, a rat is worse, but only slightly,* he thought.

Mother shrieked,

"A MOUSE! GET IT OUT OF HERE!"

The children reeled away from the table. "Get it, Father!" Griffin shouted.

"Quick!" Maggie screamed. "Catch it!"

Before Huxley could take a breath, Father was after him, swinging a cloth napkin like a whip. Huxley leapt onto Mother's lap and jumped off. As he soared through the air, he noticed Tubbs, waiting for him below.

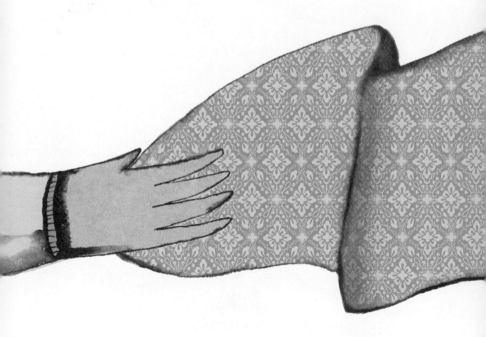

Oh, dear, Huxley thought. *This cat is a problem.*

He landed on Tubbs' head and held onto his collar as the startled beast took off. It raced through the house with Father chasing closely behind. The ground shook as the large man's black shoes crashed beside them. Tubbs darted under a stool in the kitchen and Father smashed into it, sending it flying.

A cup broke beside them. A saucer shattered. A broom swung, and its wind tumbled them over. Huxley scrambled to his feet, but it was too late. He found himself under a clear glass bowl. Father slid an envelope under him and raised it to the counter.

"You've caught him!" Griffin said.

"Nice work, Father," Maggie said.

"Get rid of it," Mother said. "I can't bear the sight of those disgusting creatures."

"Yes, yes," Father said. "Of course." Just as he reached out to pick up the bowl, Huxley knocked on the glass that imprisoned him.

Griffin grabbed his father's arm. "Look at him. What is he doing?"

Huxley took the ink bottle out of his vest and dipped his tail into it.

"He's writing with his tail," Maggie said. "Look at him."

"Good heavens," Mother said with her eyes closed.

"What does it say?" Griffin asked.

Father shook his head. "I can't tell yet."

"I can," Maggie said.

"IT SAYS 'HELLO,
I'M HUXLEY.'"

"A MOUSE THAT WRITES,"

Griffin said, beaming.

"Look at that," Maggie said. She was smiling as well.

Mother uncovered her eyes to have a peek. "I don't believe it," she said.

Father raised his eyebrows. "This is impossible."

"No, it's not," Griffin said. "Huxley's the one who wrote the notes we've found."

Maggie held up the notebook for the mouse to see. "Did you write this too?"

Huxley nodded.

"Why, that's fantastic," Father said.

"The handwriting is lovely," Mother said. "You could learn a thing or two from him, Griffin. Not to mention you, Margaret."

To Griffin's delight, Maggie grimaced.

Huxley wrote: I would be happy to help.

"Can we keep him?" Maggie asked. "He's my mouse, you know."

"He's my mouse too," Griffin said. "You have to share, Maggie."

"We can't keep him," Father said. "That's absurd. Mice are vermin, right, Mother?"

"I don't know," Mother said, smiling. "He *is* rather cute. And he could be a great help to the children with their schoolwork."

Father folded his arms and looked sternly at Huxley.

All eyes were on Huxley, who froze with fear. Then he had an idea. Huxley dipped his tail into the ink bottle and wrote: Would you like me to write you a story?

A huge grin spread across Father's face. He seemed transformed, as if he were a boy again. He lifted the bowl and gently patted Huxley on the head.

"WELCOME TO THE FAMILY, HUXLEY,"

Father said.

From that day on, Huxley no longer wrote stories just for himself. He shared them with his new family. He wrote one for Griffin. He wrote one for Maggie. He even wrote one for Tubbs. During the holidays he penned the family's greetings, taking great pride in writing the letter about what the Taylors had done during the year. He especially liked the part about discovering Huxley, the mouse writer who lives beneath the stairs.

The End